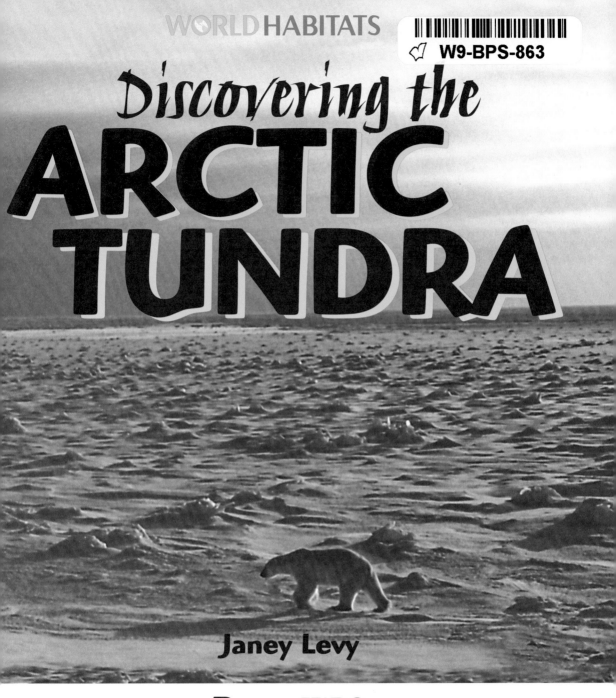

Discovering the
ARCTIC
TUNDRA

Janey Levy

PowerKiDS press.

New York

Published in 2008 by The Rosen Publishing Group, Inc.
29 East 21st Street, New York, NY 10010

First Edition

Editor: Joanne Randolph and Geeta Sobha
Book Design: Julio Gil
Photo Researcher: Nicole Pristash

Photo Credits: Cover, p. 1 © Norbert Rosing/Getty Images; pp. 5, 6, 8, 10, 13, 14, 17, 18, 25, 27, 29 © Shutterstock.com; p. 21 © George Hunter/SuperStock; p. 22 © Holton Collection/SuperStock; p. 24 © Getty Images.

Library of Congress Cataloging-in-Publication Data

Levy, Janey.
  Discovering the Arctic tundra / Janey Levy. — 1st ed.
      p. cm. — (World habitats)
  Includes index.
  ISBN-13: 978-1-4042-3787-2 (library binding)
  ISBN-10: 1-4042-3787-9 (library binding)
  1. Tundra ecology—Arctic regions—Juvenile literature. 2. Tundras—Arctic regions—Juvenile literature. I. Title.
  QH541.5.T8L48 2008
  577.5'86—dc22
                                                    2006103405

Manufactured in the United States of America

Contents

What Is an Arctic Tundra? 4

The Climate of Arctic Tundras 7

Where in the World Are Arctic Tundras? 9

Arctic Tundra Plants 12

Arctic Tundra Animals 16

People of Arctic Tundras 20

Dangers to Arctic Tundras 23

The Importance of Arctic Tundras 25

Protecting Arctic Tundras 28

Arctic Tundra Facts and Figures 30

Glossary 31

Index 32

Web Sites 32

What Is an Arctic Tundra?

A tundra is a cold, vast, treeless region. The word "tundra" comes from the word *tūnter* in the language of the Sami people. It means "treeless land." Most tundras are pretty flat, but some have mountains. Tundras have long, very cold winters and short, cool summers. The bare, rocky ground is frozen and covered with snow for much of the year. Below the surface soil is a layer of permafrost.

Arctic tundras are located in Earth's far northern regions around the Arctic Ocean. This is one of the planet's coldest places. It is also one of the driest. Arctic tundras receive less than 10 inches (25 cm) of rain annually. This means they are as dry as deserts!

Arctic tundras have existed for only about 10,000 years. This makes them the youngest biome on Earth. A biome is a community of plants and animals that live together in a region and depend on each other.

This is a shot of the arctic tundra taken during the short summer months. You can see that no trees grow on the bare, rocky ground.

Flowering plants, grasses, and sedges are just a few of the plants that grow during the summer in the Arctic tundra.

The Climate of Arctic Tundras

Arctic tundras have only two seasons, winter and summer. Winter is long, lasting from 6 to 10 months. The temperatures are extremely cold and may get as low as -50° F (-46° C) or below! Winds blowing 60 miles per hour (97 km/h) or more create even colder conditions. The winter sun stays below or barely above the horizon.

Land of the Midnight Sun

The Sun never sets for about two months during Arctic tundra summers. This period of continuous sunlight gets longer as you get closer to the North Pole. There, the Sun does not set for six months.

Summer is short, mild, and sunny. It lasts only 6 to 10 weeks. Temperatures resemble winter temperatures in the southern United States. They range from 37° F (3° C) to 54° F (12° C). There is plenty of sunlight because the Sun mostly stays above the horizon. However, the sunlight is weak, since the Sun stays low in the sky.

The tundra is covered in snow much of the year. Even during the summer, the soil that makes up the permafrost is always frozen.

Where in the World Are Arctic Tundras?

Arctic tundras cover about one-fifth of Earth's land surface. They occur in Earth's Arctic region, a very cold region around the Arctic Ocean, at the top of the world. The Arctic extends north from a line called the Arctic Circle all the way to the North Pole.

Three continents have Arctic tundras: North America, Europe, and Asia. In North America, Arctic

Alpine Tundras

Tundras can also be found on high mountain elevations where it is too cold for trees to grow. These tundras, called alpine tundras, occur in North America's Rocky Mountains, Europe's Alps, and Asia's Himalaya.

tundras cover a large part of Alaska and about half of Canada. Part of Alaska's tundra is actually below the Arctic Circle. However, because the climate matches that of Arctic tundras, scientists

Alaska's Denali National Park is made up of two biomes, the tundra and the taiga. Taiga means "northern evergreen forest."

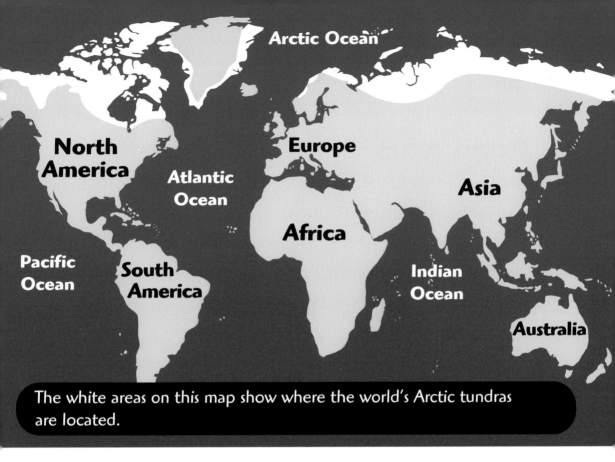

The white areas on this map show where the world's Arctic tundras are located.

consider this area to be Arctic tundra. Arctic tundra also appears along the coast of Greenland, which is east of northern Canada.

In Europe, the northern tips of Norway, Sweden, and Finland have Arctic tundra. The northern coast of the European part of Russia does also. In Asia, Arctic tundra covers much of Siberia, which is the northern part of Russia.

Arctic Tundra Plants

About 1,700 plant species grow in Arctic tundras, including 400 kinds of flowering plants. Arctic tundra plants include shrubs, mosses, grasses, sedges, and lichens, unusual plants that are actually a combination of algae and fungus.

Arctic tundras' cold temperatures, strong winds, short growing season, weak sunlight, and permafrost strongly affect plants. The plants that grow there have adapted to these harsh conditions.

Arctic tundra plants are small, short, and grow clumped together to resist the wind and gain protection from the cold. Being close to the ground allows them to benefit from heat captured by the soil in summer. Many plants also have hairy leaves that hold in heat. Other plants have dark red leaves that take in more heat from the Sun than green

The orange and yellow growth on this tree is lichen. Lichen is able to grow in places where most plants and animals could not live.

leaves do. The bowl shapes of many flowers collect light and heat.

Plants must grow rapidly because of the short growing season. They must be able to perform photosynthesis at low temperatures and in weak sunlight. Tundra plants actually begin photosynthesis in early summer while they are still covered with snow! They use less energy than plants in other biomes, so they do not need to produce as much. Because of the permafrost, plants must have shallow root systems.

A Warm Blanket

You probably think of snow as something harmful to Arctic tundra plants. However, the snow is actually warmer than the Arctic air above it. It acts like a blanket that protects the plants.

Pasque flowers are one of the flowering plants that can live on the tundra. The hairy flowers are also dark in color to hold in heat.

Arctic Tundra Animals

Like Arctic tundra plants, tundra animals must adapt to the fierce conditions of the tundra. Many animals migrate to the tundra. They come in summer to breed and enjoy the tundra's rich variety of food. They move south for the winter. Animals that remain through the winter have special features.

Most Arctic birds, including ducks, snow geese, tundra swans, some falcons, and loons, migrate south for the winter. Snowy owls, ptarmigan, ravens, and some falcons remain. They have special feathers to protect them from the cold. Ptarmigan even have feathers on the bottom of their feet! The feathers of snowy owls and ptarmigan change colors with the seasons to hide them from enemies.

Most mammals remain through the winter, although some reindeer migrate. Arctic mammals include Arctic foxes, wolves, grizzly bears, polar

This snowy owl's feathers have turned white for the winter. During the short summer, the owl's feathers are brownish with dark stripes and spots.

bears, reindeer, and musk oxen, which are related to goats. There are also weasels, including ermines, and many rodent species, including ground squirrels, hares, lemmings, and voles, and shrews.

The animals have thick fur to keep them warm. Some have thick layers of fat. Many have short legs, small ears, and short tails to prevent heat loss through

Some Very Special Fur

Reflected light makes a polar bear's fur appear white, but it is really clear. This allows sunlight to reach the bear's black skin, which takes in heat from the sunlight to help keep the bear warm.

those body parts. Ground squirrels and grizzly bears hibernate. Some mammals have fur that changes color with the seasons.

Animals also swim in icy Arctic waters. Fish include cod, salmon, and trout. Mammals include seals, whales, and walruses. Arctic tundras even have insects. Mosquitoes, flies, moths, grasshoppers, and bees live there.

These harbor seals make their home on the icy waters off the coast of Alaska. They eat shellfish and many different kinds of fish.

People of Arctic Tundras

Many groups of people live in Arctic tundras. Some have lived there for as long as the tundras have existed, or about 10,000 years. Alaska's Arctic tundra people include Inuit, Aleuts, Inupiat, and Yupiks. Inuit also live in Canada and in Greenland. In Europe, the Sami people, sometimes called Lapps, live in northern Norway, Sweden, Finland, and Russia. Asian Russia's Arctic tundra people include Yupiks, Nenets, and Khanty.

For centuries, these groups practiced similar ways of life.

Inuit Homes

Many people think that all Inuit of the past lived in snow houses called igloos. However, only the Inuit of Canada used igloos. Some used them on hunting trips. For others, igloos were winter homes made by covering regular homes of earth and animal skins with ice blocks.

This Inuit man makes his living hunting seals. He still uses tools like those used by Inuit seal hunters long ago.

These Inuit children peek out from under a polar-bear skin. While some things have changed for the Inuit, many of their old ways of life remain.

Extended families shared homes in small communities. They hunted and fished and moved with the change of seasons. They valued sharing and working together. They respected the land and the animals that lived there.

Life has changed greatly for Arctic tundra people in the last few centuries. Many now live in one place all year. Some, such as the Sami, now farm and herd reindeer. Others have moved to cities. In spite of all these changes, Arctic people try to maintain their ancient values and way of life.

Dangers to Arctic Tundras

Arctic tundra people, animals, and plants have adapted to live in the particular conditions of Arctic tundras. Even small changes can harm Arctic tundras and have a big effect on life there.

Mining and drilling for oil and natural gas pollute the air and water, harm the permafrost, and take land away from Arctic tundra animals. An accident or oil spill can cause damage that could never be repaired. Mining and drilling also bring people who build towns and roads that harm the permafrost.

Lasting Marks

Footprints and tire tracks in the tundra can cause a lot of harm. As sun hits the prints or tracks and melts the permafrost, these marks become larger. Tracks made in World War II, fought from 1939 to 1945, have become so large that some of them are now lakes.

Oil spilled from an oil tanker washes up on the beach. Oil spills kill countless animals, fish, and plants.

Global warming also presents dangers. It raises the temperature and melts the permafrost and sea ice. Plants and animals adapted to Arctic tundras cannot live in the warmer climate and may vanish. The traditions of native Arctic people, who depend on the animals for food, may vanish as well.

The Importance of Arctic Tundras

Arctic tundras are so far away and have such small numbers of people and of plant and animal species that it may seem like they are not very important. However, that is not true.

Arctic tundras are home to some of the world's most unusual animal species. Without the tundras, these animals would vanish. Many migrating birds

An Arctic tern has caught a fish. Arctic terns breed in the Arctic and then travel south, all the way to Antarctica, before heading back to the Arctic.

that spend most of the year in other biomes depend on Arctic tundras for breeding and rearing their young. Without the tundras, these birds would disappear.

Global warming affects Arctic tundras more quickly than it affects other biomes. Changes in the Arctic tundras may be an early warning signal that global warming is becoming great enough to cause major changes to Earth. Moreover, changes to Arctic tundras caused by global warming may affect the entire planet.

Arctic tundras trap and store carbon dioxide. This gas increases global warming. As Arctic tundras become warmer, they will release this carbon dioxide into the air.

Permafrost can preserve dead plants and animals for a very long time. Scientists can study these remains to learn more about Earth's past.

Polar bears depend on the icy Arctic tundra to live. The bears may disappear if temperatures keep rising due to global warming.

Protecting Arctic Tundras

Many people are working to protect Arctic tundras. One way is to set aside parks or other special areas. Another way is to use less energy. Using lots of electricity as well as driving a lot contribute to global warming. They also encourage people to drill for oil in Arctic tundra areas. Here are some things you can do to reduce your use of energy:

- Turn off lights, computers, and TVs when you are not using them.
- Turn down the heat.
- Take shorter, cooler showers.
- Take a bus, ride your bike, or walk.
- Do not buy products with lots of packaging. It takes energy to make all that packaging.

Arctic tundras need our help. We must work together to protect them.

The Arctic tundra is a beautiful and important biome. It is our job to keep the plants and animals of this biome safe. What will you do to help?

Arctic Tundra Facts and Figures

- Pools of water cover Arctic tundras in summer since melting snow cannot seep through permafrost.

- Footprints and tire tracks remain visible for many years.

- Global warming has heated the Arctic more than any other biome.

- Arctic tundra plants grow at colder temperatures than any other plants.

- Flowers turn to follow the Sun's movement so they get as much light and heat as possible.

- Polar bears can smell food 20 miles (32 km) away.

- An adult polar bear's stomach holds more than 150 pounds (68 kg) of food.

- To stay warm in winter, nose bot flies go into reindeers' noses.

- The Inuit call musk ox Oomingmak, which means "bearded one."

- Inuit do not like the name "Eskimos." They prefer "Inuit," which means "the people" in their language.

Glossary

algae (AL-jee) Plantlike living things without roots or stems that live in water.

carbon dioxide (KAR-bin dy-OK-syd) A gas that plants take in from the air and use to make food.

fungus (FUN-gis) A living thing that is like a plant, but that does not have leaves, flowers, or green color, and that does not make its own food.

hibernate (HY-bur-nayt) To spend the winter in a sleeplike state.

mammals (MA-mulz) Warm-blooded animals that have a backbone and hair, breathe air, and feed milk to their young.

migrate (MY-grayt) To move from one place to another.

photosynthesis (foh-toh-SIN-thuh-sus) The way in which green plants make their own food from sunlight, water, and a gas called carbon dioxide.

ptarmigan (TAHR-mih-gun) Ground-dwelling birds that live in northern regions.

rodent (ROH-dent) An animal with gnawing teeth, such as a mouse.

sedges (SEJ-ez) Grasslike plants that grow in soil covered by shallow water.

species (SPEE-sheez) A single kind of living thing.

temperatures (TEM-pur-cherz) How hot or cold things are.

Index

A
algae, 12
animals, 4, 16, 19, 22–23, 25–26
Arctic Ocean, 4, 9

B
biome(s), 4, 15, 26

C
carbon dioxide, 26

D
deserts, 4

F
fungus, 12

G
ground, 4, 12

L
layer(s), 4, 19

M
mammals, 16, 19
mountains, 4

P
permafrost, 4, 12, 15, 23, 26
photosynthesis, 15
plants, 4, 12, 15–16, 23, 26
ptarmigan, 16

R
rain, 4
region(s), 4, 9

S
Sami, 4, 20, 22
season(s), 7, 12, 15, 19, 22
snow, 4, 15
sunlight, 7, 12, 15

T
temperature(s), 7, 12, 15, 23

W
winds, 7, 12

Web Sites

Due to the changing nature of Internet links, PowerKids Press has developed an online list of Web sites related to the subject of this book. This site is updated regularly. Please use this link to access the list: www.powerkidslinks.com/whab/tundra/